This book belongs to

Anne Gilbey

I have always loved horses. As a child I rode them, cared for them,
*read about them and was always drawing them. Writing **Sea Horse**,*
I wanted to capture that special bond between a child and a horse.
I also wanted to tell a story about following your dreams, venturing
into the unknown, which may be both exciting and unsettling.
At the heart of this story, though, is the instinctive feeling
that whatever the distance between us and those we love,
there is a bond that will always endure.

Sally Millard – this book was always for you
K. L.

First published in Great Britain in 2012 by
Gullane Children's Books
185 Fleet Street, London, EC4A 2HS
www.gullanebooks.com

1   3   5   7   9   10   8   6   4   2

Text and illustrations © Karin Littlewood 2012

ISBN: 978-1-86233-829-6

Printed and bound in China

Sea Horse

by Karin Littlewood

GULLANE
CHILDREN'S BOOKS

For as long as they could both remember,
the boy had his horse.
And the horse had his boy.

It seemed as if it would be this way for ever.

Each night the horse would wait in his stable for the boy to come.
And the boy had a shell.
In the silence of the shadows they heard
the sounds of the wild wild waves and the songs of the sea,
and they would listen to the shell as it told them stories of distant oceans.

But the story the horse loved the most was the one that
told of the great white horses, with their flowing manes
and thundering hooves, dancing in the waves.

He was filled with a deep longing and would dream of
galloping with them – running wild and free.
The feeling grew until the horse could wait no longer.
He had to join them.

So that night the boy quietly opened the stable door and,
holding the shell, led the horse out into the darkness.

The moon shone a gleaming path upon the earth.
High above, a white owl in its silent flight hooted gently.

They rode past sleeping towns and hidden villages,
through twisted valleys and over rounded hills.
On and on . . .

And the shell sang softly.

But now the path led them into a tangled forest, and soon they were lost in
its inky darkness. The horse gave a deep sigh and the cry of a fox echoed back:
"I will lead you in and out of the shadows."

They followed her amber eyes to the far side.
And the shell's song was strong and clear.

By dawn they reached the open hills. "Which way now?" cried the boy.
Leaping and bounding a hare appeared:
"I can take you to the edge of the brown fields."

In the clear morning light, they flew across the land.
And the shell's song grew louder.

Now the fields dropped down to a broad clear river.
Silvery fish leapt and splashed in its waters.
"Soon, soon, at the river's end,
soon you will be there," they called.

The horse trembled and quivered
and the boy gripped the shell.

The shell sung as if it would burst.

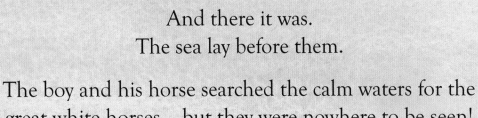

And there it was.
The sea lay before them.

The boy and his horse searched the calm waters for the
great white horses – but they were nowhere to be seen!

They gazed along the shore and waited and waited
until the sky was filled with its evening glow.
Again and again the shell told the story the horse loved the most . . .

until it could sing no more.

The horse hung his head.
His dream was over.

He walked slowly away, his heavy hooves
leaving deep prints in the sand.

But a gentle breeze now ruffled the air.
Behind them the sky began to darken.

As the boy took one last glance towards the sea,
he cried out – "Look around you!" The horse looked up . . .

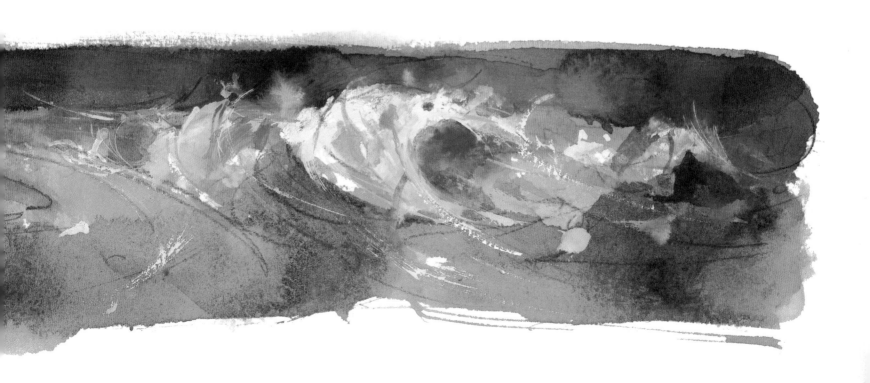

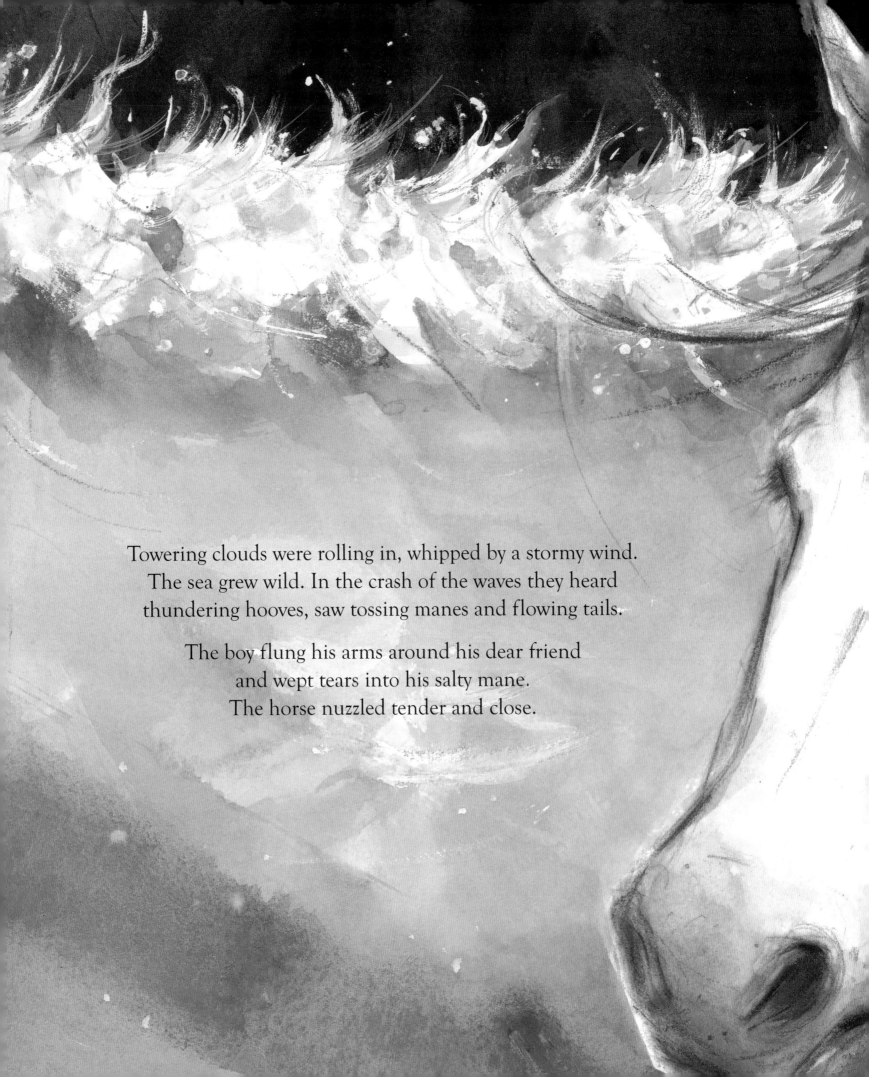

Towering clouds were rolling in, whipped by a stormy wind.
The sea grew wild. In the crash of the waves they heard
thundering hooves, saw tossing manes and flowing tails.

The boy flung his arms around his dear friend
and wept tears into his salty mane.
The horse nuzzled tender and close.

And the great white horses rose from the sea!

They were calling him. Gently the horse pulled away and, with a flick of his tail, he was off, galloping into the wild waves to join them.

For a long time the boy looked out to sea.

Then a stillness touched the air and the waves were calmed.
And, in the quiet, the boy turned and began his journey home.

The boy still has his shell.
He listens to the songs of the sea and the stories of distant oceans.
But now the shell has a new story and he loves this one the most,
for it tells of a boy and his horse.

He smiles a quiet smile. Hidden deep in the sounds of the faraway waves
he can hear *his* horse calling as he gallops in the tumbling waters.
Forever wild and free.

And that's the most beautiful sound of all.

Other books from Karin Littlewood

Immi

One day, Immi finds a colourful wooden bird at the end of her fishing line. The next day she finds a red flower, followed by an orange starfish. But where do these bright gifts come from? And who can Immi thank for the joy they have given her?

"One of the most understated and beautiful picture books of the year"
BOOKSELLER

"A story with a quiet magic and beauty"
PUBLISHERS WEEKLY (Starred Review)

The Most Important Gift of All
WRITTEN BY David Conway

What gift can Ama give her new baby brother?
The gift of love, says Grandma Sisi. So Ama goes in search of love, asking every animal she meets – until eventually, with her father's help, she realises its source lies very much closer to home...

"Achieves the timelessness of an ethnic myth"
BOOKTRUST

"Exquisite"
SCHOOL LIBRARY JOURNAL

Nominated for the KATE GREENAWAY MEDAL

Moonshadow
WRITTEN BY Gillian Lobel

Moonshadow is travelling south for the first time.
Led by Grandfather, the swans fly over sleepy cities and shimmering seas. But suddenly tragedy strikes –
and Moonshadow's future is destined to change for ever...

"Outstanding storytelling"
SCHOOL LIBRARY JOURNAL

"Enchanting illustrations fill each page"
CHILDREN'S LITERATURE